Leo the Late Bloomer

BY ROBERT KRAUS • PICTURES BY JOSE ARUEGO

Simon and Schuster Books for Young Readers
Published by Simon & Schuster Inc., New York

For Ken Dewey

and

For Pamela, Bruce and Billy

Text copyright © 1971 by Robert Kraus
Illustrations copyright © 1971 by Jose Aruego
All rights reserved including the right of reproduction
in whole or in part in any form.
Published by Simon and Schuster Books for Young Readers
A Division of Simon & Schuster, Inc.
Simon & Schuster Building
Rockefeller Center
1230 Avenue of the Americas
New York, NY 10020

10 9 8 7 6 5   pbk

Originally published by Windmill Books, Inc.
Simon and Schuster Books for Young Readers is a
trademark of Simon & Schuster, Inc.
Manufactured in the United States of America

Library of Congress Cataloging-in-Publication Data
Kraus, Robert, 1925–
   Leo the late bloomer / by Robert Kraus : pictures by Jose Aruego. p. cm.
   Summary: Leo, a young tiger, finally blooms under the anxious eyes of his parents.
   [1. Tigers—Fiction.] I. Aruego, Jose, ill.
II. Title.
PZ7.K868Le 1987 [E]—dc19 87-30191 CIP AC
ISBN 0-671-66271-6

Leo couldn't do anything right.

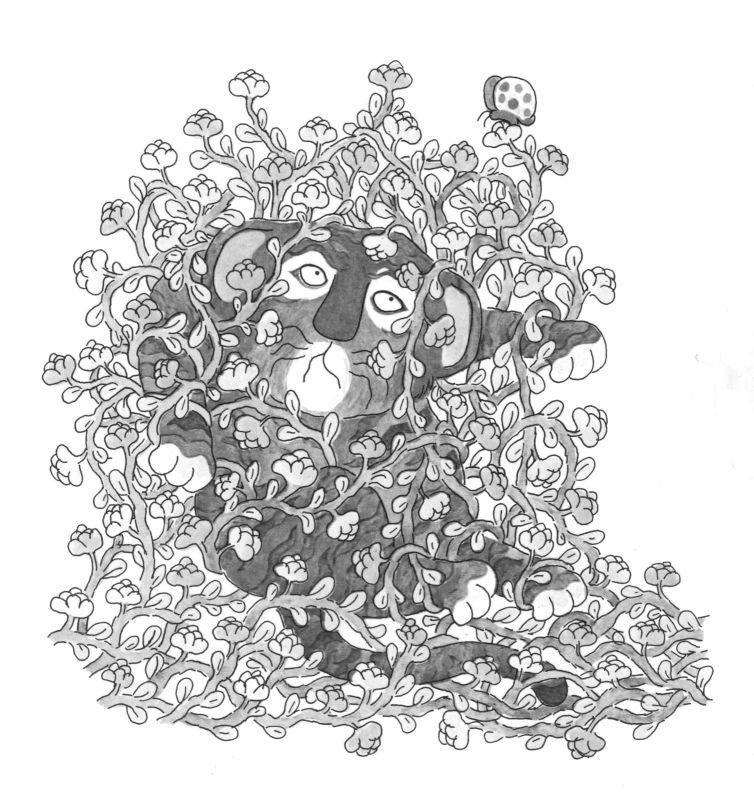

He couldn't read.

He couldn't write.

owl
Elephant
Snake
Plover
Crocodile

He couldn't draw.

He was a sloppy eater.

And, he never said a word.

"What's the matter with Leo?"
asked Leo's father.
"Nothing," said Leo's mother.
"Leo is just a late bloomer."
"Better late than never," thought Leo's father.

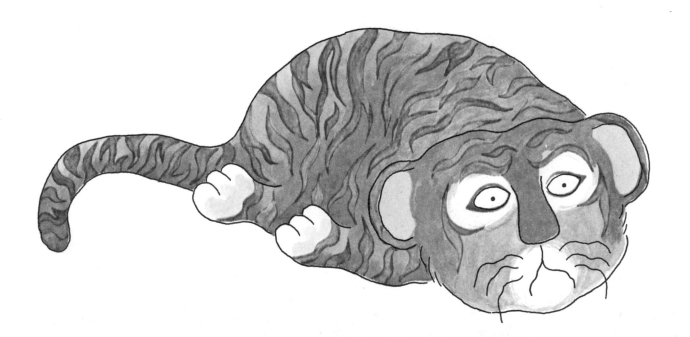

Every day Leo's father watched him for signs of blooming.

And every night Leo's father watched him
for signs of blooming.

"Are you sure Leo's a bloomer?"
asked Leo's father.
"Patience," said Leo's mother,
"A watched bloomer doesn't bloom."

So Leo's father watched television
instead of Leo.

The snows came.
Leo's father wasn't watching.
But Leo still wasn't blooming.

Then one day,
in his own good time,
Leo bloomed!

He could read!

He could write!

He could draw!

He ate neatly!

He also spoke.
And it wasn't just a word.
It was a whole sentence.
And that sentence was...

"I made it!"